This Walker book belongs to:

_____

_____

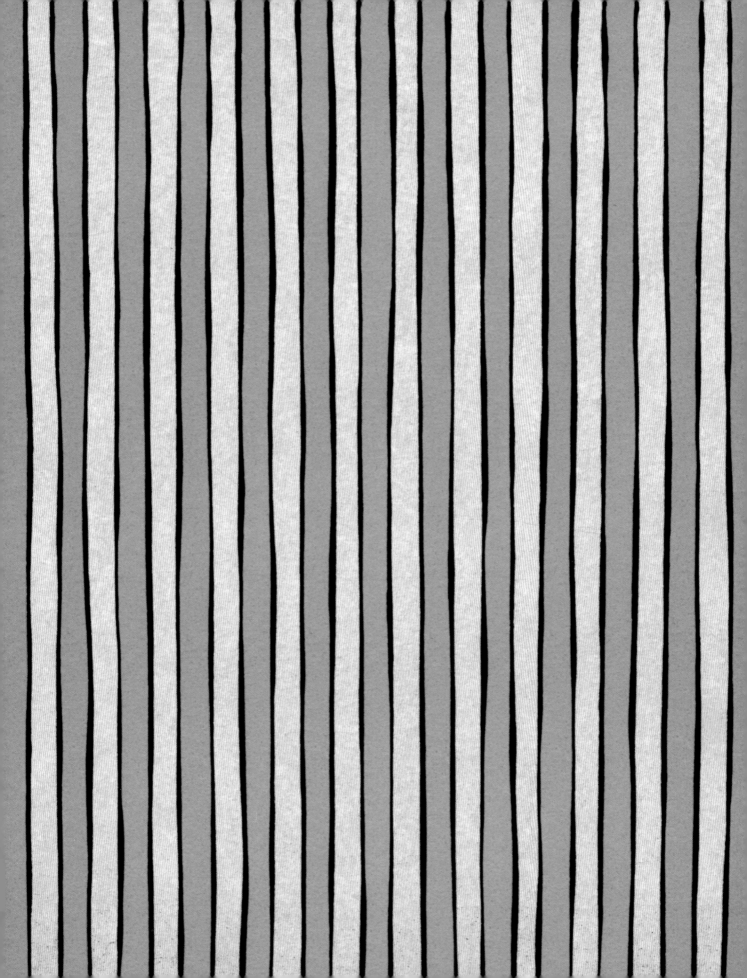

Text first published 1986
by HarperCollins Publishers Ltd
First published in 1994
by Walker Books Ltd
87 Vauxhall Walk
London SE11 5HJ

This edition first published 2008

2 4 6 8 10 9 7 5 3 1

Text © 1986 Judy Hindley
Illustrations © 1994 Nick Sharratt

The moral rights of the author
and illustrator have been asserted.

This book has been typeset in Garamond Book Educational.

Printed in China

British Library Cataloguing in Publication Data:
a catalogue record for this book is available.
from the British Library

ISBN 978-1-4063-1668-1

www.walker.co.uk

Little and Big

Judy Hindley

Illustrated by
Nick Sharratt

WALKER BOOKS
AND SUBSIDIARIES
LONDON • BOSTON • SYDNEY • AUCKLAND

Tall, tall, tall –

a very tall wall.

We feel small

near the very tall wall.

This wall is not tall.

This wall is low.

Off we all go

on the wall that is low.

Who is up high?

Who is down low?

Perhaps we should stay

on the wall that is low.

Perhaps we should climb

on the wall that is tall?

No, no!

Watch out!

It's far too high.

It's not safe to go there

unless you can fly.

Here's my friend, Sam.

Is he short?

Is he tall?

Is he wide?

Is he thin?

Is he big?

Is he small?

He's not as tall

as the wall.

He's not as tall

as the tree.

He's not as big

as a house

or a tower

but he is much taller

and bigger

than me!

And I am much bigger

than my friend Jane,

and Jane is much bigger

than Fred.

And Fred is

much, much, much, much,

much bigger than his friend,

Bugsy the Red.

Bugsy the Red?

Who's he?

Is he big?

Oh, no!

Is he tall?

He is not!

He is little,

and tiny,

and small.

But he can fly high,

way up in the sky,

higher up

than that very tall wall –

and the kite and the house

and the tree.

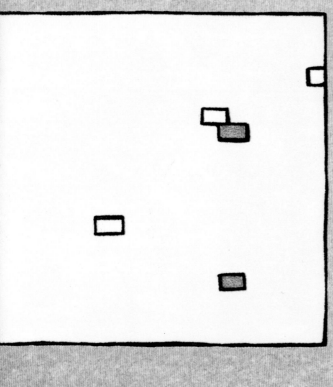

Oh, no!

He's heading down

for a fall.

CRASH!

Quick! Let's go for a ride.

Let's go down a road that is wide.

Come, let us go

through a tunnel I know,

if we can all fit inside.

Oh, oh, oh!

This tunnel's too low!

No, we will NOT fit inside!

Come, let us try

a tunnel that's high.

Hurray!

It's as high as a tree!

Oh, dear!

I'm afraid

this tunnel was made

for someone much

thinner than me.

We need a tunnel

as wide as a bus.

Oh, where is the tunnel for us?

Whee!

That was the one for us!

Now let us all go home

to our homes that are little and big.

The one that is tall,

and the one that is small,

and the one that is short and wide.

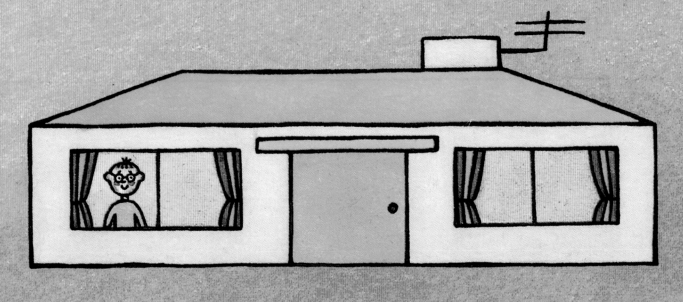

Which home

do *I* fit inside?

This one is just

the right size.

Bye bye!

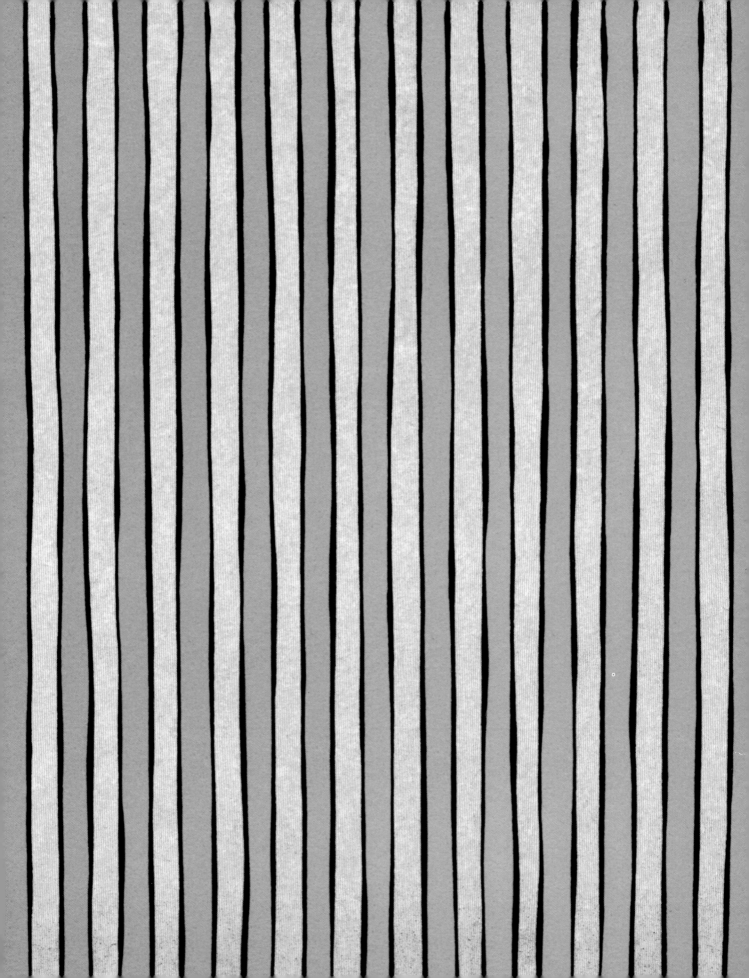

Titles in this series

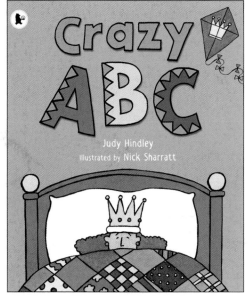

Crazy ABC
Judy Hindley
Illustrated by Nick Sharratt

ISBN 978-1-4063-1669-8

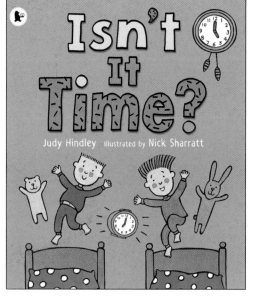

Isn't It Time?
Judy Hindley   Illustrated by Nick Sharratt

ISBN 978-1-4063-1670-4

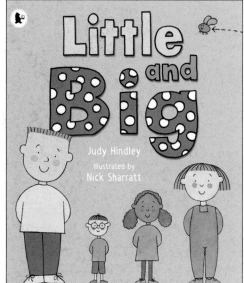

Little and Big
Judy Hindley
Illustrated by Nick Sharratt

ISBN 978-1-4063-1668-1

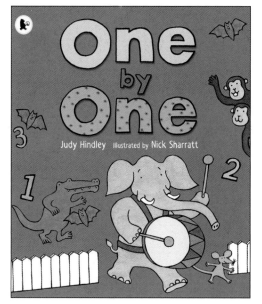

One by One
Judy Hindley   Illustrated by Nick Sharratt

ISBN 978-1-4063-1667-4

Available from all good bookstores

www.walker.co.uk

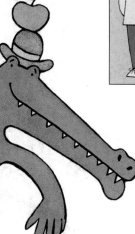